Mike and the Mighty Shield

by HIT Entertainment

Simon Spotlight

New York London Toronto Sydney New Delhi

SIMON SPOTLIGHT
An imprint of Simon & Schuster Children's Publishing Division
1230 Avenue of the Americas, New York, New York 10020
© 2013 Hit (MTK) Limited. Mike the Knight™ and logo and Be a Knight, Do It Right!™ are
trademarks of Hit (MTK) Limited. Nickelodeon and all related titles and logos are trademarks
of Viacom International, Inc. All rights reserved, including the right of reproduction in whole
or in part in any form. SIMON SPOTLIGHT and colophon are registered trademarks of
Simon & Schuster, Inc. For information about special discounts for bulk purchases, please
contact Simon & Schuster Special Sales at 1-866-506-1949 or business@simonandschuster.com.
Manufactured in the United States of America 0413 LAK
First Edition 10 9 8 7 6 5 4 3 2 1
ISBN 978-1-4424-7431-4
ISBN 978-1-4424-7432-1 (eBook)

Here's Mike the Knight,
a fine young lad,
who wants to be
just like his dad.
So Sparkie and Squirt
will take the field
beside young Mike
and his mighty shield!

Mike the Knight spotted a painting of his dad on the Glendragon Castle wall.

"Look at Dad bouncing Vikings off his shield!"

"That's how knights test their shields," explained the queen. "Vikings love bouncing almost as much as they love jam tarts!"

This gave Mike an idea. "I'll try bouncing with my shield! Not with real Vikings, of course. But I know two dragons who will help."

Mike and his friends Sparkie and Squirt ran down the tower steps together, headed outside. On the way down, Mike spotted the shield from the painting.

"Hmmm," said Mike. "What if my shield isn't best? I'll try bouncing with this one instead."

Sparkie lifted the mighty shield down. "Are you sure, Mike? It's very heavy."

"All I need is a little practice. By the king's crown, that's it! I'm Mike the Knight and my mission is to bounce Vikings with the greatest shield in all of Glendragon!"

Mike raced to his bedroom and pulled the secret handle to put on his armor.

"I'm ready for action," he said, returning outside and drawing his sword. At the end of the sword, Mike got a surprise. "A jam tart?"

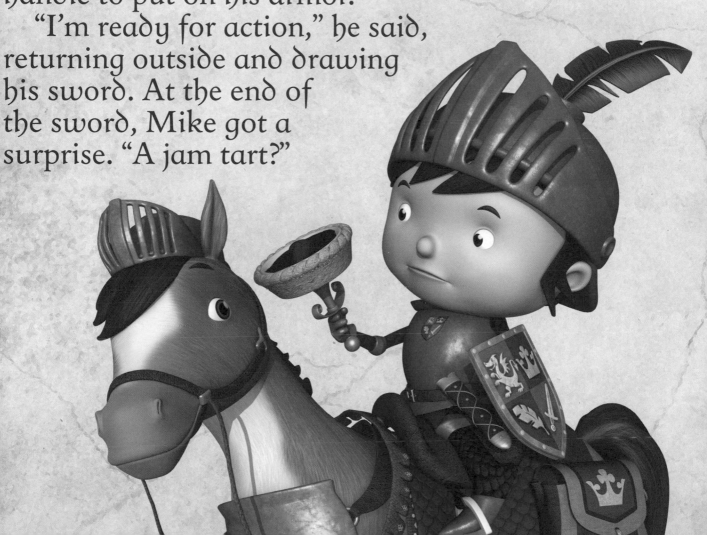

Mike was so excited to try his dad's shield! "Squirt, now that I have a new shield, you can have my old one!" he offered. "But look, Mike!" Squirt said. "Your old shield has a button—wow! It makes it bigger."

"My new, mighty shield has *lots* of buttons. It is the biggest and the best shield ever!" declared Mike.

But when Mike tried to lift his new shield, it was too heavy for him.

"Could you carry this to the beach for me, Sparkie? I'm, um, saving my strength."

When they reached the beach, Sparkie handed the mighty shield to Mike, who wobbled under its weight.

"Just getting my balance," Mike mumbled. "Okay, Sparkie. If you run at me, I'll try bouncing you off of my shield."

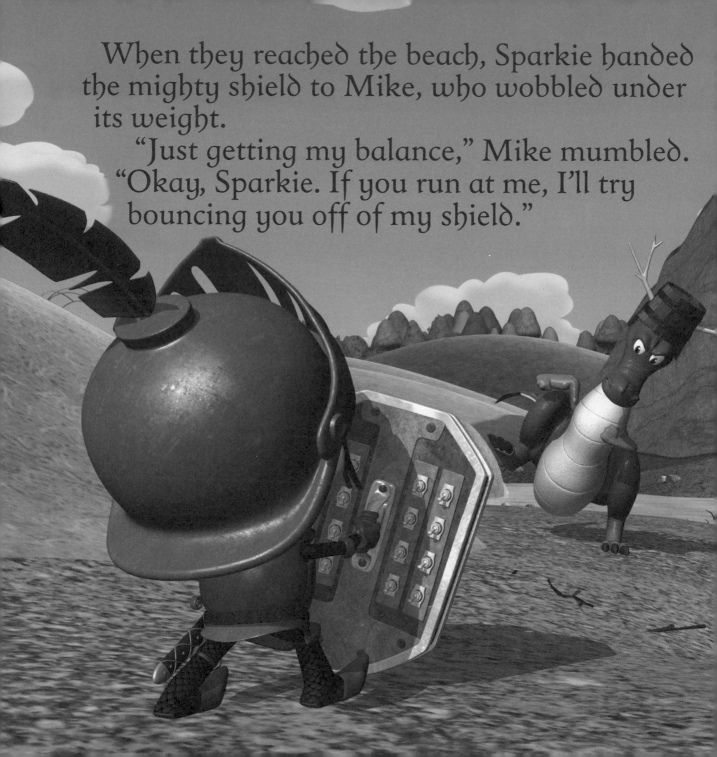

Sparkie, wearing his special Viking hat, ran toward Mike, but Mike couldn't see over the mighty shield and fell over!

"Are you sure you don't want to use your old shield, instead?" asked Sparkie. "We could trade."

While Mike and Sparkie were practicing on the beach, they didn't notice a Viking ship out at sea.

"You need to be more like a Viking, Sparkie. That's the problem," said Mike, as he propped up the shield. "Vikings are noisy, they do somersaults, and they crash into things!"

The Vikings heard Mike and rowed toward the shore.

Sparkie stomped along the beach and did a somersault while he shouted "Øøørg! Snørg! Høørgh!" just like a Viking.

The Vikings heard Sparkie and rowed even faster toward the shore.

Meanwhile, Squirt was on the other side of the beach, practicing how to hold his new shield. He could even throw it in the air and catch it!

Squirt was bouncing imaginary Vikings off his shield when the real Vikings jumped off their boat and tried to grab it.

"Help!" he cried, trying to keep the shield away from the Vikings.

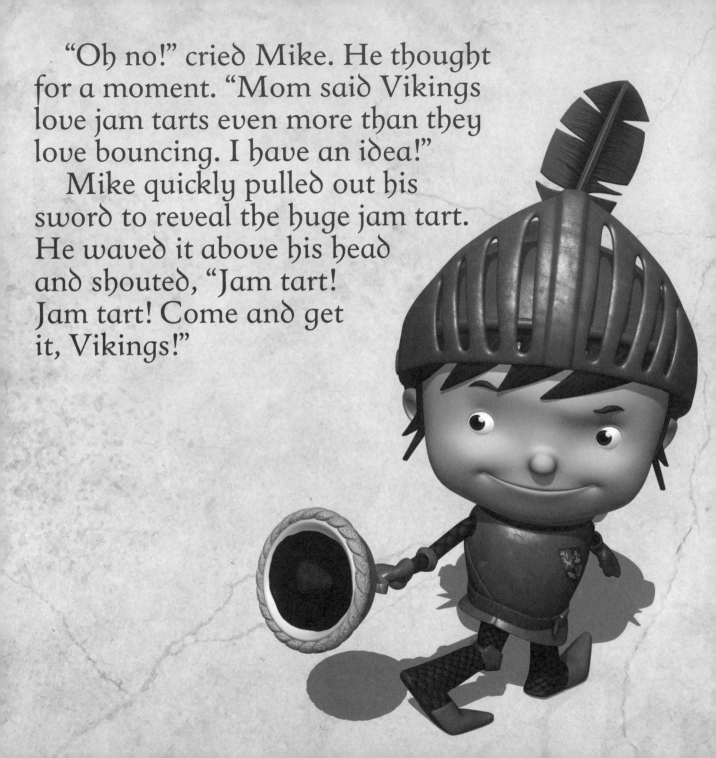

"Oh no!" cried Mike. He thought for a moment. "Mom said Vikings love jam tarts even more than they love bouncing. I have an idea!"

Mike quickly pulled out his sword to reveal the huge jam tart. He waved it above his head and shouted, "Jam tart! Jam tart! Come and get it, Vikings!"

The Vikings spun around. "Jøøm tøørt! Jøøm tøørt!"

Mike flung the jam tart far away from Squirt, and the Vikings ran after it.

Now that the Vikings stopped bothering Squirt, Mike had a question for his friend, "I'm sorry, Squirt, but Dad's shield is too heavy for me," Mike said. "May I have my old shield back?"

"Yes, take it! I can't keep it away from the Vikings!" Squirt said happily. "But by any chance do you have any more jam tarts, Mike?"

"No, but I do have my shield, and it's time to **be a knight and do it right!**" Mike shouted.

It was time to bounce some Vikings.

The Vikings were so excited when they saw the shield "Shøøøld! Bøøørgh!" they said, as they bounced on the ground.

"Do you think your little shield will bounce them?" asked Sparkie.

"I have to try," Mike said.

Mike pushed the button on his shield to make it bigger. "Come on shield! Please bounce for me!"

The first Viking ran at Mike's shield and bounced perfectly. Then the second and third Vikings bounced perfectly too.

Mike held his shield and bounced each Viking straight back into their boat. Sparkie quickly pushed the boat off the beach and it floated out to sea. At last, all the Vikings were gone!

Back at the castle, Sparkie helped Mike put the mighty shield back where it belonged.

"I see you've found one of your father's old shields," Queen Martha said. "He never liked that one . . . it was far too big and heavy to bounce Vikings!"

"That's funny, Mom!" Mike said, laughing. "That's just what I thought. I guess my shield is the best shield for me, after all!"